CHRISTMAS AT A GRAND HOTEL

To Abigail + Grace,
Jesus loves you!
Wini Frances
10/27/2012

BY WINI FRANCES

WinePress **Kids**
Great Books, Defined.

WinePress Kids
Great Books, Defined.

To order additional copies of this book call:
1-877-421-READ (7323)
or please visit our website at
www.WinePressbooks.com

If you enjoyed this quality custom-published book,
drop by our website for more books and information.

www.winepresspublishing.com
"Your partner in custom publishing."

To my wonderful mother, Charlotte Fagen,
and my loving husband, Mike
Thanks for all your support and encouragement.

I can do all things through Christ who strengthens me.
—Philippians 4:13, NKJV

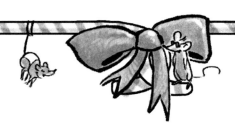

Charlie, a small gray field mouse, stood by his mother and gazed at the huge polished wooden staircase curving up as far as he could see. Fresh greenery and twinkling white lights draped the railings. His long, silky whiskers twitched as he wiggled his nose and inhaled the scents of pine and holly. It smelled like Christmas.

His bright eyes sparkled when he spied a giant gingerbread house in the center of the lobby. His mouth watered and he licked his lips as he stared at the yummy pink frosting curtains and red licorice shutters at the windows. The front door of the house, trimmed in green gum drops, opened with a red and white striped candy cane handle. Charlie's tummy rumbled as he eyed the chocolate candy kisses stuck in the thick white icing of the roof.

"Oh, Mama, everything is just beautiful!"

Mama bent down and patted his head. "Now don't touch anything. Stay right here in the corner by the curtain. I'm going to help Papa bring the suitcases and gifts inside. Please watch your little brother. Don't let him wander away."

When Mama walked away, Charlie sneaked a peek around the corner. His mouth dropped open. The huge room had a high domed ceiling with colorful patterns of lights dancing across it. Millions of little shiny squares in a rainbow of colors formed stunning designs on the floor. Christmas trees circled the room. And one giant tree stood right in the middle reaching over halfway to the top of the dome.

Some trees twinkled with bright white lights. Blue lights glowed on a tall white tree covered with silver ornaments.

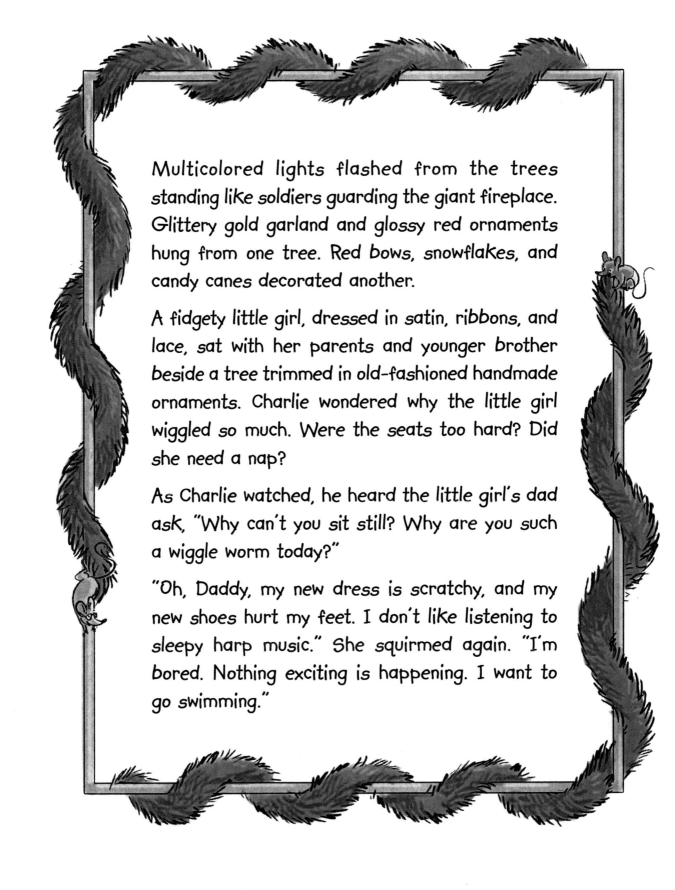

Multicolored lights flashed from the trees standing like soldiers guarding the giant fireplace. Glittery gold garland and glossy red ornaments hung from one tree. Red bows, snowflakes, and candy canes decorated another.

A fidgety little girl, dressed in satin, ribbons, and lace, sat with her parents and younger brother beside a tree trimmed in old-fashioned handmade ornaments. Charlie wondered why the little girl wiggled so much. Were the seats too hard? Did she need a nap?

As Charlie watched, he heard the little girl's dad ask, "Why can't you sit still? Why are you such a wiggle worm today?"

"Oh, Daddy, my new dress is scratchy, and my new shoes hurt my feet. I don't like listening to sleepy harp music." She squirmed again. "I'm bored. Nothing exciting is happening. I want to go swimming."

Her father hugged her close. "Sit still a few more minutes. And when the concert is over I'll take you and your brother to the pool." The little girl smiled up at her father, folded her hands in her lap, and tried her best to sit still.

Just then, Charlie heard a sound like a tennis shoe squeaking on a gym floor. Uh oh! He'd know that squeak anywhere. He'd forgotten all about being responsible for his little brother, Sam. Charlie had been more interested in watching all the people and staring at the magnificent decorations in the huge domed room than taking care of his little brother.

Charlie turned toward the squeak and gasped. He watched, horrified, as Sam bounced along the carpeted hallway, stuck to a dangling Velcro strap attached to a large red duffle bag.

A little boy skipped down the hall dragging the red bag behind him, unaware of Sam's problem.

Charlie raced after his little brother. A wide-eyed Sam kicked his feet and waved his arms as he twisted and turned, trying to break free. Charlie ran faster and leaped to grab Sam's tail just when two ladies wearing long fancy gowns stepped from the gift shop. Oh no! Their swishing dresses captured him and pulled him under. He found himself in a dark circle, being swept this way and that down the hall like a dust mop.

The ladies hurried around the corner, and their dresses swayed sideways. Charlie saw a sliver of light and darted through the opening. Whew! Free at last! He stopped and looked all around, but could not see the little boy with the duffle bag anywhere.

From the other side of the room a little boy shouted. "Mommy, come see the donkey."

Charlie ran toward the voice. Could this be the little boy he was looking for? He rounded the corner and almost crashed into a live nativity scene. The people and animals looked just like the picture in his Bible storybook. A woman knelt in the straw next to the manger. A man stood beside her gazing down. A donkey munched on hay, while the sheep slept nearby.

The little boy pranced around, pointing at the donkey lying in the straw. But where was the duffle bag? Charlie sighed with relief when he spied it lying against the manger where Baby Jesus slept. Then he groaned. An empty strap dangled from the big red bag.

With legs shaking and tail twitching, Charlie scurried around hunting for Sam. He looked under the manger. No Sam. He crawled between the sheep. No Sam. He lifted the end of the donkey's tail. No Sam. Mama and Papa would be back soon and be very upset if Charlie lost Sam. He tunneled under the straw. "Sam! Sam! Where are you?" Charlie listened hard. A moment later he heard a faint whisper coming from over his head.

Charlie made sure nobody was watching before he scampered up one of the manger legs and peered over the top. There lay Sam. His chest heaved, and he gasped for air as he lay sprawled in the straw next to Baby Jesus.

Charlie leaned way over and whispered, "Sam, are you okay? How did you get in there?"

Sam blinked back tears and breathed a heavy sigh. "I followed you when you peeked in the big room. A boy dragging a monster red bag headed straight for me. He would have smashed me, if I hadn't run close to the wall to get out of his way. But a sticky strap brushed over me and stuck to my fur. I thought I had been caught in one of those new mouse traps Mama warned us about."

"But how did you end up in here?"

"When the boy tossed his bag next to the manger leg, I dug my claws into the wood and held on. I finally popped loose and climbed to the top."

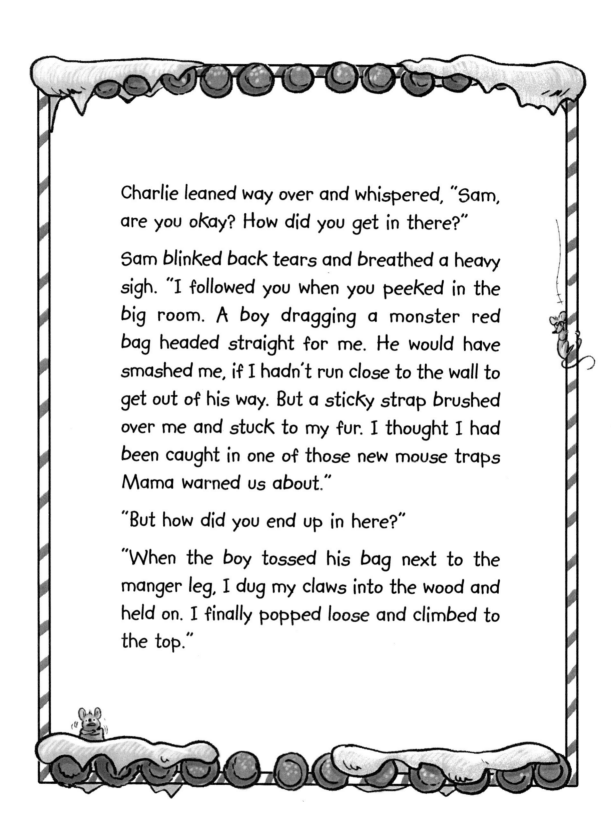

"Then I looked over the edge and saw Baby Jesus. I thought if a manger is a safe place for Baby Jesus, it's safe for me too."

"Grab my tail and hang on, Sam. I'll pull you out of there. We're going to be in big trouble with Mama and Papa if we don't hurry."

Sam snatched Charlie's tail and hung on tight. Charlie dashed down the manger leg and hid them both in the straw. While Charlie planned what to do next, he heard the mother of the little boy with the red bag telling the story of Baby Jesus.

"Do you remember Jesus was born in a manger over 2000 years ago in a city called Bethlehem?"

"Yes. And they didn't have cars."

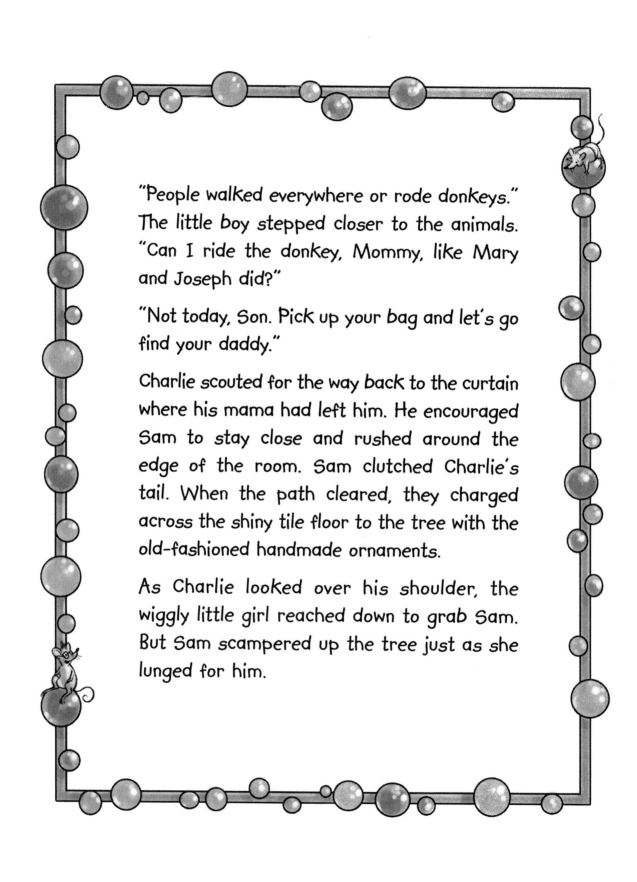

"People walked everywhere or rode donkeys." The little boy stepped closer to the animals. "Can I ride the donkey, Mommy, like Mary and Joseph did?"

"Not today, Son. Pick up your bag and let's go find your daddy."

Charlie scouted for the way back to the curtain where his mama had left him. He encouraged Sam to stay close and rushed around the edge of the room. Sam clutched Charlie's tail. When the path cleared, they charged across the shiny tile floor to the tree with the old-fashioned handmade ornaments.

As Charlie looked over his shoulder, the wiggly little girl reached down to grab Sam. But Sam scampered up the tree just as she lunged for him.

Panting for breath, he teetered on a branch and fell off. Charlie heard the little girl laugh and watched with gaping mouth as Sam somersaulted through the air. He crashed through the branches, catching his heels on a strand of popcorn and swinging back and forth several times before diving into a stocking hanging on a lower branch. Ornaments clattered to the floor. Some shattered. Others rolled away.

The little girl clapped her hands and danced around until her father scowled at her and told her to sit down. Sam took that opportunity to escape from the stocking and sprint to Charlie. Off they went again, scurrying to the corner where their mother had left them.

They slid from behind the curtain just as Papa and Mama walked over.

"Whew!" Charlie whispered. "We just made it!"

Mama leaned over and patted both of her boys. "I'm *so* glad you are such good little mice. Because you stayed out of trouble while I helped Papa, later this evening we will take you to see the sights. I especially want you to see the live animals by Baby Jesus in the manger and hear about the miracle of His birth."

Mama hugged them close. "All the decorations and gifts are wonderful, but I want you to know the true meaning of Christmas. God's greatest gift to us—the birth of His son, Jesus, is what Christmas is all about. Remember the Bible story Papa reads every Christmas morning?"

"I remember," Sam said. "We heard the...." Charlie tugged Sam's tail to shush him.

"Mary gave birth to Jesus in a stable, not a hospital. She wrapped Him in a blanket and laid Him in a manger with clean straw. He had to sleep with the animals because there was no room for his parents, Mary and Joseph, in the inn."

Charlie grinned at Mama. "That's right. Bethlehem was full of people. They had to go back to their family's hometown to be counted by the government and to pay taxes."

Mama smiled back at Charlie, proud he had listened when Papa read the story. "What a special night!" Mama continued. "As the shepherds were in the field at night watching over their sheep, an angel appeared and announced the birth of Jesus. He told them not to be afraid. Then the heavens filled with more angels than they could count, all of them praising God."

"The animals in the stable also knew this was no ordinary night. The sheep. The cows. The donkey. And even some of our relatives watching from their hiding places in the straw."

Charlie's mind wandered back to that scene over two thousand years ago. *What would it have been like to have been there on that first Christmas night so long ago? It would have been even more exciting than our trip to the manger.*

Sam tugged on Charlie's arm and whispered. "The manger was a safe place for Baby Jesus and a safe place for me. Being with Jesus keeps everyone safe."

Charlie nodded and gave his brother a great big hug. "Merry Christmas, Sam."

CPSIA information can be obtained at www.ICGtesting.com
Printed in the USA
LVOW110621171012

303128LV00006B/1/P